Fertile for the Forbidden Billionaire

Willow Watkins

Copyright Page

❤

Contents

Chapter One

Rose

I slam the trunk of my car shut a little harder than I intend to and instantly regret it. The whole thing rattles like something might fall off completely, and I cringe. The last thing I need is my car breaking down on me, too.

I step back and wipe a sweaty palm down my jeans. The sun is beating down, and my shirt is clinging me to in a way that makes me feel gross and uncomfortable. My hair is a mess, and I'm pretty sure I smell like a sad blend of stress, sweat, and despair.

This is the lowest I've ever felt.

Chase dumped me last night after giving him six months of my life, all because I wouldn't put out for him. But then maybe I would have done if I'd felt like he was actually serious about me. If he hadn't always been flirting with other women right under my nose and then acting like it was nothing. My only regret today is that I hadn't ended things with him before he got a chance to.

And now, this morning, I'm having to move out of my apartment, thanks to a burst pipe from the apartment above that ended up flooding my bathroom. The landlord didn't offer to help me find a new place. He didn't even give me a timeline of how long it might be before I can move in again.

And I have nowhere to go.

None of my friends have space, and I'm too proud to ask anyone twice. I have about twenty dollars to my name and two weeks left of my college classes before finals. And now I'm mentally preparing to live in my car for a few days or weeks while I figure my shit out.

The worst part? I almost called Chase this morning. I almost begged him to take me back just so I might have somewhere to stay.

But I didn't. No matter how low I might have fallen, I still have a little pride left.

Even if it's buried somewhere under the boxes stacked in my backseat. I didn't want to leave all my stuff behind in case the water damage got even worse, so my stay in my car is going to be more than a little cramped.

I sigh and reach for the final box on the sidewalk. Then I hear it.

The low expensive purr of an engine.

A sleek, black car slows to a stop at the curb just behind mine. My heart stutters as I register whose car it is.

Damien Knight's.

My ex-boyfriend's brother.

The older brother. The responsible one. The serious one. The one who inherited the entire damn tech security empire that their father built.

And the one I've secretly crushed on since the very first time I met him.

He steps out of the car like he's walking onto the set of a luxury watch commercial - tailored charcoal pants, crisp white shirt, but no tie today. He's also gone without the suit jacket, no doubt thanks to the heat. His sleeves are rolled up just enough to reveal powerful forearms, his jaw is sharp enough to cut through glass, and his dark hair is a little mussed, like somebody has been running their hands through it all day.

The jealousy that rises up inside me at that thought is both irrational and inappropriate, so I do my best to push it down.

"Rose?" His voice is deep, smooth, just slightly rough. Like velvet over gravel. "What's going on?"

I freeze with the box still in my arms and instantly want the ground to open up and swallow me whole. I probably look like a wreck.

"Ummm..." I shift awkwardly. "My apartment flooded. Burst pipe. I have to move out while they fix it."

His eyes flick to the pile of boxes on the back seat of my car. "Where are you going?"

I hesitate. There's no way I'm going to tell him about the fact that I'll be living in my car for a while. I have no doubt that Chase will find it hilarious if he hears about it.

"It's just... temporary. I'll be fine."

If I expect to dodge his question with that non-answer, I'm quickly proven wrong when he narrows his eyes and fixes me with an intense stare.

"Temporary where?"

I hate that his presence makes my stomach flutter. I hate that I suddenly care that I'm wearing old sneakers and have my hair in a messy bun, with a few escaped strands sticking to my sweaty forehead.

I hate how much I want to cry again, all because he's looking at me like he actually cares about where I go.

"I'll figure it out," I mumble, brushing past him towards my car.

But he steps in, gently taking the box from me. His fingers brush against mine briefly, and I swear I feel my knees almost buckle from that small amount of contact. And then he's turning to the trunk of his car - not mine - and sliding the box inside it.

"Damien, what are you...?"

"You're not sleeping in your car, Rose," he interrupts, his voice firm enough that I know it's probably not wise to argue. "It's not safe."

"How did you...?"

"I just know," he says smoothly. "And it's not happening. I won't allow it."

He grabs another one of my boxes like it weighs nothing - one that I've been dragging like a corpse for the last ten minutes - and carries it back to his car without breaking a sweat.

I stare for a few moments, enjoying the sight of such masculine strength. He's broad-shouldered, and the muscles beneath his shirt are defined and toned. The way he moves is effortless, but there's a raw power in him that makes him impossible to ignore.

I know better than to let myself get caught up in thoughts like that, but right now I'm a little too tired and frazzled to control myself.

"Seriously, I'm fine. You don't have to do this."

"Stop." His voice is even firmer now. He turns back to face me, arms crossed over that broad chest. "You're staying at my place. Just until things get fixed here. It's non-negotiable."

I blink. "I can't impose on you like that."

"You can. You will. I'm not asking."

He's not... mad. But he's serious. Like boardroom-dominating, no-room-for-argument serious. The kind of serious that makes me feel a little lightheaded and entirely too warm between my thighs.

I hate how much I like this bossy side of Damien.

"But won't the whole thing with Chase just make this all feel awkward? You know he broke up with me last night, right?"

His jaw tics, just barely, and his eyes narrow slightly at the mention of his younger brother.

"I know. Which means you don't have to answer to him anymore. You're free to move in with me for a while."

I nod. "Okay."

Just like that, with one word, I'm letting Damien freaking Knight take me home.

As we work together to move all my things into his car, although realistically, he is doing a lot more heavy lifting than I am, I tell myself that it's only for a few days. Just until I figure something else out. Just because he's being kind.

But as I climb into the passenger seat of his car, my hands trembling and my body reacting in ways I don't understand, one thought echoes in my mind:

I'm in so much trouble.

Chapter Two

Damien

Rose moves around my kitchen like she's always belonged here. Barefoot, hair piled on top of her head in a messy knot, sleeves rolled up as she stirs something on the stove. A soft hum slips from her lips as she works, and it's only now that I realize how silent my home usually is. Too silent.

And I sit at the kitchen table like a goddamn statue, pretending to check emails on my phone when I haven't read a single word in ten minutes. All I've done is stare.

She insisted on making dinner as a thank you for letting her stay with me, as if I wouldn't give her the entire world if she asked for it. As if she has to earn a damn thing from me.

Watching her here, in my house, filling it with warmth and the smell of garlic and butter and something sweet underneath, I swear I've never felt more content. She's only been here for a few hours, but it already feels like something inside me has shifted.

I like having her in my space. No. I love it.

The sheer domesticity of it all hits me harder than I expected. It's not just about how good she looks - though she does, standing here in my kitchen wearing one of her little sundresses, the hem teasing the top of her thighs. It's the fantasy that sinks deep into my bones.

This is what I want.

Rose. Here. Every night. Every morning. Cooking in my kitchen and sleeping in my bed. Getting rounder with my baby and never, ever worrying about a damn thing again.

I want her barefoot and pregnant, living in the lap of safety and pleasure. I want her swollen with my child and glowing from being worshipped.

And I want her to know that I've been waiting - burning - for the chance to take care of her the way he never could.

I always knew my younger brother was too immature for her. Incapable of giving her everything she deserves. They are both twenty-one, but she's mature. She needs someone older, like me, who at thirty-five years old can offer her the kind of stability and protection that a man like Chase can't.

For six long months, I kept my distance. Watched from the sidelines while she dated my brother. Bit back my obsession and swallowed the need every time she smiled at me across a family dinner table. Because she was off-limits. She was his.

But now?

Now she's single, and she's right here. Under my roof. And even though she's trying to pretend this is just temporary, we both know it isn't.

Well, I do. And if Rose hasn't worked that out for herself yet, she will do soon enough.

I can't let her go. Not after the utter fear I felt when I saw her piling boxes into her car this morning. My first thought had been that she was leaving town after her breakup with Chase, although it hadn't taken me long to realize it was simply a maintenance issue making her leave.

Not much scares me. But the idea of losing Rose, or of something happening to her, fucking terrifies me.

That was why I'd found out who her landlord was the day after meeting her for the first time, offering him an insane deal on one of my newest set of security cameras in and around the apartment building where she lives. It was an offer he couldn't refuse, although I would have offered to install them for free if he had done that. She knew the cameras were there, although I have no idea if she knew it was my company that installed them.

And that was how I'd known she was in trouble this morning. Even though it's wrong, I've been using those cameras to keep tabs on her for the last few months, making sure she's safe.

As soon as I'd realized there was an issue, I'd dropped everything at work and rushed to her. There was no way I was going to let her sleep in her car or end up on the streets. Not when I'm around to take care of her.

"Dinner's almost ready," she says softly, glancing over her shoulder with a shy smile. "I hope you're hungry."

"For you?" I murmur before I can stop myself. "Always."

Her cheeks flush, and she turns back to the stove quickly. "I meant for the food."

"I didn't."

I let the silence fill the room for a moment too long before clearing my throat and leaning back in my chair. "So... are you going to tell me what happened?"

Her shoulders tense. "What do you mean?"

"With Chase." I keep my tone even. Calm. "Why did you two break up?"

She hesitates before answering. "We just... weren't working."

I raise a brow. "That's a politician's answer."

Rose lets out a humorless laugh. "It's complicated, that's all."

"I've got time."

She moves to the counter, plating up food, her hands suddenly trembling slightly. "I really don't want to get into it."

"Rose," I say, my voice still soft, but with a firmer tone that lets her know I expect a real answer. "Tell me."

She pauses and then sighs, looking over at me with a pretty blush staining her beautiful face. "He wanted something from me that I wasn't ready to give."

I don't say anything. I simply arch a brow and wait for her to elaborate, which she thankfully does after a few seconds.

"He wanted sex. But I hadn't... I haven't done that before. So I wanted my first time to be special. I want it to mean something to the person I'm with. But he was always flirting with other girls. He didn't even try to hide it. And I didn't want to give something so special to someone who was doing that."

My fingers curl into fists under the table. Even the triumph I feel at finding out that she's still untouched isn't enough to dampen the rage that coils like a viper in my chest. My fucking brother tried to pressure her into having sex.

The very idea of him - of anyone - laying a finger on her without her consent is enough to make me want to murder someone.

"And what happened when you told him no one too many times?" I ask, forcing my voice to stay steady.

She lifts one shoulder in a small shrug. "He said I was being immature. That he didn't want to wait around forever."

I push my chair back and rise to my feet.

Rose looks up, startled, just as I reach her.

"I... Damien, are you okay?"

No.

I'm nowhere near okay.

I step in close. Close enough to make her breath hitch, to see the flutter of her pulse in her throat. I don't touch her. I won't. Not until she asks. But I back her up until she's against the edge of the counter, my arms braced on either side, caging her in.

"I'm sorry he made you feel like that," I say, my voice low and quiet, dark with everything I'm holding back. "You deserved more that he ever could've given you."

Her lips part, but no sound comes out.

"You deserve someone who'll worship the ground you walk on," I murmur. "Someone who'd wait forever just to kiss you. Someone who'd give you every damn thing you want just to see you smile."

I lean in until my forehead brushes hers. "You deserve someone who sees you as everything, Rose. Not just a conquest. Not a prize. But his entire fucking world."

She's trembling, and each breath that leaves her body emerges on a soft little whimper that has my dick straining painfully inside my pants.

"Someone like you?" she whispers.

My eyes drop to her lips, and it takes every bit of willpower I possess not to close the distance between us completely. To claim those pretty lips as mine for the very first time.

"Yes," I say, my voice showing no hint of doubt or hesitation. "Someone exactly like me."

Because it's always been me, and soon, she's going to know that down to her very soul.

I take a step back, feeling the absence of her closeness like a physical ache in an instant.

"Come on," I say, my voice a little rough, still heavy with need. "Let's eat."

She blinks a couple of times, looking dazed, and then nods. She slides past me, careful not to brush against me, and walks towards the table, carrying our plates.

And if I let my gaze linger on her perfect ass for a few moments longer than is strictly necessary?

Well, it's not my fault. She's too beautiful to ignore.

And now I know what it feels like to have her close, there's no way I can just walk away from her.

I want her.

And I will make her mine.

Chapter Three

Rose

I've been staring at the same sentence for twenty minutes.

The words blur on the page, my textbook growing heavier in my lap the longer I sit here pretending like I'm actually studying for finals. I shift on the bed, let out a sigh, and close the book with a soft thud. Who am I kidding? There's no way I'm focusing today. Not after last night.

Everything since dinner has been a blur.

I keep replaying Damien's voice in my head, deep and controlled, but laced with something sharp and possessive underneath. Like he was barely holding himself back. Like if I'd just moved a little closer, he might have touched me.

He didn't, though.

He didn't touch me. He didn't kiss me.

He just stood there with that heat burning in his eyes, said things that turned my entire world upside down... and then walked away like he hadn't just rocked the foundations of everything I thought I knew.

It's crazy. There's no way he actually meant what I think he meant.

Right?

I mean, Damien Knight is a billionaire. Powerful, important, busy. Men like him don't want someone like me. They don't look at their brother's broke, freshly dumped ex-girlfriend and think - she's mine.

Still, the way he'd spoken to me. The way he looked at me.

I shiver at the memory, goosebumps rising along my arms. I've never felt like that before. Never been looked at like that before.

But this is all wrong. I was dating his brother until literally two days ago. What would Chase think of me if he knew I was living with his oldest brother? And the rest of their family? I have no doubt they would be disgusted by the very thought of it.

Giving up any attempt at being productive, I toss my textbook onto the bed and stand, pacing a little before wandering towards the bedroom door. Damien's at work, and the house is quiet and still around me. He'd told me to treat the place like my own, and given how restless I'm feeling, maybe a little bit of exploring will help.

My fingers trail along the wall as I walk. The house is stunning, but it's also warm. Lived in. Somehow, even though everything is modern and luxurious, it doesn't feel cold. It feels like him. Masculine. Strong. Steady.

Each of the doors is open, revealing one guest bedroom after another. Only one door remains closed, the one at the end of the hallway, and I know before I reach it what must be hiding behind the wooden panels.

Damien's bedroom.

I hesitate for half a second, but curiosity gets the better of me. I push the door open slowly.

It's exactly what I expected. Dark woods. Deep gray linens. Clean lines. Everything neat, of course - except for a single shirt tossed over the back of a chair near the window. A black button-down.

I step inside the room like I'm crossing into something sacred, my eyes wide as I glance around, like I'm trying to soak up every little detail. Every little thing that might give me more of a clue about the kind of man Damien is.

I shouldn't be in here. I know that. But I can't help myself.

I walk towards the chair, my entire body tingling with nerves as I reach out and pick up the shirt. It's soft in my hands, but large - like him. I bring it to my nose before I can stop myself and breathe in.

God.

I close my eyes.

He was wearing this. It smells like him. And something about it makes my whole body ache.

Without thinking, I tug my t-shirt over my head and shimmy out of my shorts. I don't know what I'm doing or why. Or maybe I do, and I'm just not willing to admit it to myself. My bra and panties are the final items to be added to the pile of clothing at my feet.

I slip the shirt over my bare skin.

It hangs off my body like a robe, swallowing me in fabric and his scent. I roll the sleeves a couple of times so I can see my hands. Something clenches deep in my stomach, and my nipples harden almost instantly, the sensitive buds sending little jolts of pleasure through me as they rub against the soft cotton.

I walk towards his bed on shaky legs, then crawl across the comforter and lie back against his pillows.

Everything in here is Damien. All of it.

And now I'm wrapped up in him. Surrounded by him. Just like I'd dreamed about last night.

My thighs press together, and my breath hitches.

I think about the conversation last night. About the way his voice dropped when he said I deserved someone better. Someone like him.

I think about how his body felt as he'd cornered me, making me feel small and wanted and owned all at once, without even a single touch.

What would it be like if he gave in to temptation and actually touched me?

My hand slides down my body, my breath catching in my throat as I imagine Damien's voice, low and rough, whispering that I belong to him. That no one will ever touch me but him.

That he'll be the one to make me scream. To make me come.

I'm wet, aching, and desperate as my fingertips dip lower, brushing against my soaked folds, finding the sensitive little bundle of nerves hidden between them.

My head tilts back, my eyes closing as a little gasp falls from my lips.

My fingers circle my clit.

I think about him walking through the door, finding me in his bed like this.

His hands spreading my thighs.

His weight on top of me.

His lips on my skin.

I imagine the way his thick, hard cock would feel as it presses inside me. How it would stretch me open, inch by inch, until it's filling me so deeply I can't move. I dip two fingers inside my slick opening, sliding them in and out in a way that has me moaning, and yet I still know he'd be able to make it feel so much better.

I imagine the way his mouth would taste. His tongue.

My fingers pick up their pace.

I'm so close.

So close.

So...

"Oh God."

The words leave me in a rush, and then I'm coming. Hard. My entire body tightening and arching, my fingers moving faster, chasing every single moment of pleasure.

And all the while, Damien's name is on my lips, silent and sweet and desperate.

My chest rises and falls as I lie there, the pleasure slowly fading as the realization of what I've done hits.

I just got off in Damien Knight's bed.

To thoughts of him.

But somehow, it wasn't enough. The ache between my thighs is still just as intense as it was before, and I have a feeling I won't know what true satisfaction feels like until the first time he touches me.

But as I bring my hand back between my thighs, I'm determined to try.

Chapter Four

♥

Damien

The boardroom is a blur of suits, voices, and graphs that mean nothing to me right now.

I'm supposed to be listening. I should be focused. There's a quarterly report on the screen, numbers ticking up and down, charts being analyzed. Someone at the far end of the table is talking about projections for the next quarter. I nod like I'm paying attention, but I couldn't care less.

All I can think about is her.

Rose.

The way she looked last night, standing in my kitchen like she belonged there. The soft gasp she made when she realized I want her. The way she looked up at me when I pinned her to the counter and told her she deserves more.

That sweet little blush. Those wide eyes. The way she trembled.

She's mine. I just haven't claimed her yet.

And it's driving me insane.

Without thinking, I slide my phone into my lap and angle the screen just enough so no one else can see it. I flip through the feeds from the security cameras back at my house - living room, kitchen, hallway.

Nothing.

Disappointment starts to rise up in my chest. I want to see her. Just a glimpse. Maybe she's curled up on the couch reading a book. Maybe she's making coffee or a snack.

Part of me knows that there's a chance she's decided to hide out in her bedroom for the day, in which case I won't see her. The only bedroom in my home with a security camera in it is mine, because of the safe I have hidden in the closet. But I can hope that maybe she's making herself at home and I might get to see her for just a moment.

As I flick past the feed from my bedroom, it takes me a moment too long to realize there was a movement on the camera, and I have to swipe back.

I stop breathing.

She's on my bed.

Wearing my shirt.

Sprawled out across my sheets like a fantasy I've had a thousand times.

And her hand is between her thighs.

My lungs tighten, the air catching in my throat. Blood rushes south so fast it's almost painful. I grip my phone tighter, angling it slightly so the guy closest to me can't catch sight of what's on my screen.

Because this beautiful, seductive vision is for me, and me alone. If I get my way, nobody but me will ever see her like this for the rest of my days.

Rose arches slightly. Her lips part. She's mouthing something - soft little moans, or maybe even my name.

I can't hear a damn thing and thank fuck for that. I've got the volume off, and I'm grateful that nobody else can hear her. The sounds she makes when she comes belong to me, and the longer I watch her, the harder it is not to just walk right out of the meeting so I can rush home and hear those sounds in person.

Multiple times. Until she's completely sated and can't come anymore.

My hand clenches beneath the table. I'm rock hard and aching now, barely able to sit still, trying to keep my breathing even while some asshole from accounting drones on about return on investment.

I glance up once, pretending to engage, giving a slight nod that hopefully passes as agreement. Then I'm right back to the screen.

She's moving faster now. Her hips shift, her head tips back. When she pulls the front of my shirt open, I catch sight of one pert and perfect tit for a moment before her free hand is on it, teasing the nipple with frantic fingertips. I can see the flush in her cheeks even on the small screen. She's panting. Writhing. Lost in the moment.

Lost in me.

Because that's what this is. I know it. She could have chosen any bed, any room. But she chose mine. My shirt. My scent. My space.

She wants me.

And soon, I'm going to prove to her just how badly I want her in return.

By the time the meeting ends, I'm a split second away from snapping. I don't even hear the closing remarks. I just stand, collect my things, and walk out without a word.

I need to get home.

I need to see her. Right. Fucking. Now.

And then I'm going to explore her body and find all the ways to make her scream my name. I'm going to make her forget that any other man but me exists.

Because from now on, Rose belongs to me.

Every sight. Every smile. Every moan.

Every. Damn. Inch.

Chapter Five

Rose

My legs feel a little shaky as I come down the stairs.

I'm fully dressed now, but my skin still tingles with heat, with guilt, with a need I can't seem to chase away. Every breath I take still tastes like Damien - his scent, his shirt, the thought of his hands on me even though he's never touched me.

God. What's wrong with me?

I've never done something like that before in someone else's bed. And it wasn't just anyone's bed. It was his. Damien's.

I don't understand why I can't stop thinking about him, or why my body reacts to him so intensely. Every word he's said to me ever since I moved in with him is seared into my memory, making me want things with him that I really shouldn't want with my ex-boyfriend's brother.

But he's the complete opposite of Chase in every way. Solid. Serious. Fierce. Where Chase used to forget to text me for days, Damien looks at me like I'm the only thing in the room that matters. Maybe even in the entire world.

It's addictive. Intoxicating. Dangerous.

I reach the bottom step, still trying to calm the whirlwind inside me, when a sharp knock at the front door cuts through the silence in Damien's large house.

My heart jumps.

Is it Damien?

No, of course it isn't. Why would he knock the front door of his own damn house?

I walk over to the door and pull it open, peeking out to see who it is. And then I freeze.

"Hey, Rosie."

It's Chase.

His smile is lazy and smug as he leans casually against the door frame. He doesn't say anything, just stares at me.

Like he's waiting for me to invite him in.

Something in the pit of my stomach turns. He is the last person I expected to see, and anxiety makes my chest tighten as I wonder what he must think about seeing me here. And, even worse, what he might start telling others about it.

"What do you want?" I ask, keeping my voice flat.

"Relax. I just stopped by to drop off some papers for Damien." He holds up a plain white envelope for a second, and when he lowers it again, his gaze slides over me. Head to toe. Like he's taking in every little detail about my appearance. It makes my heart race, but not in the same way Damien does. This feels a lot more unpleasant.

"I didn't expect to see you here, though, Rosie." He continues to look at me in a way that makes me uncomfortable, and when I stay silent, he continues. "Guess my big brother's into collecting my leftovers now."

The words hit me like a slap. My spine stiffens, but I don't look away. Deep down I think I always knew there was an asshole hiding under all his charm, but the callous way he says that is still a shock.

"I'm not a leftover," I spit back through gritted teeth.

Chase shrugs. "Whatever helps you sleep at night, Rosie. It's just funny, is all - how you couldn't stand the idea of sleeping with me, but now you're playing house with him?" He tilts his head to the side as he examines me. "You putting out for Damien now? Is that what you have to do to be allowed to stay here? Act like a whore and the big, bad billionaire will let you live in his house?"

Tears sting the corners of my eyes before I can stop them. I blink hard. I won't give him the satisfaction of seeing me cry.

"Leave, chase," I whisper, not trusting myself to say any more than that in case I can't hold back the tears.

"Did I touch a nerve, Rosie? I guess that means you are letting my brother bang you."

A shadow falls across the porch.

"Go ahead, Chase. Keep talking. I fucking dare you."

Damien's voice is ice cold, and the look on his face is murderous. He stands behind his younger brother, his body rigid and tense, and the anger pouring off him is palpable.

Chase's posture stiffens just slightly, but his cocky grin doesn't falter. "Look who's back."

Damien steps forward until he's towering over his brother. "Say another word about her and I'll forget we share blood. Understood?"

The tension between the two men is almost too much to bear. They stare each other down, the air between them practically vibrating.

I can't look away.

"Fine," Chase finally says, holding his hands up in a gesture of mock surrender. "I was just here to drop these papers off. No need to get all territorial. I guess I never thought a virgin like her would be a good enough lay to get someone like you pussy whipped, brother."

Damien takes the envelope from him with a sharp motion, then shoves him hard, making Chase stumble before he finds his feet again. "Get off my property. Now."

Chase hesitates and throws one last look my way, as if he's considering saying one last thing before he leaves. But then Damien steps between us, his back blocking my ex from view, and I hear footsteps as they move away.

I take a step back and Damien walks into the house, the front door clicking shut behind him.

He turns to me, breathing hard, his eyes still burning with fury. "What else did he say to you?"

I shake my head. I don't want him to know what Chase said.

Damien takes a step towards me, and I move backwards instinctively, bumping against the wall. He takes another step, then another, until there's barely a breath of space between us.

"Rose," he says, his voice a little softer, but still hard and intense. "I can see you're upset. Tell me what he said to you."

"It's nothing." I look away, not wanting to meet his eyes.

The words come out more broken than I mean them to. I feel cracked open, embarrassed, confused. Humiliated by Chase, shaken by Damien's intensity and the way he was so quick to defend me against his own flesh and blood.

It's all too much. I don't know what to feel. I don't know what I want.

Damien reaches out and cups my cheek in his hand, his touch so gentle for someone so large and powerful. It's like he's afraid he'll break me. My heart stutters in my chest, and I know if I stay here, I'll break down in front of him.

"I need space," I blurt out. "Please."

I slide out from the space between him and the wall and rush upstairs, not turning to see the look on his face. I slam my bedroom door shut and twist the lock before my legs give out beneath me.

The tears come as soon as I hit the bed.

I don't think I've ever been as confused as I am now.

All I know is that I've never wanted someone the way I want Damien.

And that scares me more than anything after everything his brother put me through.

Chapter Six

♥

Damien

For a split second, I just stand there. Torn between the need to go after Chase and make him pay for hurting my woman like this, and the need to go to Rose and comfort her.

She's halfway up the stairs, her voice cracking, her steps frantic - and I freeze. My fists are clenched at my sides, and my jaw is locked so tight it hurts.

She asked for space. Told me she needed time. And every instinct in me is at war with itself, because I want to respect what she's asking for.

But I also want to take care of her. To hold her. To wipe away those goddamn tears and swear she'll never have to cry tears of pain again. Not while I'm still breathing.

The second I hear her door slamming closed, I move.

Fuck space.

I take the stairs two at a time, my chest tight, my body thrumming with need, with frustration, with a kind of raw helpless rage I haven't ever felt before. And when I reach her door and hear the muffled sound of her crying on the other side, I completely lose it.

"Rose," I call out, my voice hard and low. "Open the door."

She doesn't respond.

My palm hits the wood, hard. "Rose, I'm not going anywhere. You don't get to hurt alone. Not while I'm here."

Still nothing but quiet sniffles that feel like a blade twisting in my ribs. The need to hold her in my arms is like a physical pain.

I lean in, lowering my voice. "If you don't open this door right now, I'll break it down. I swear to God, baby, you don't want to test me on this."

There's a beat of silence, and then the sound of a lock turning.

The second the door cracks open, I'm there.

I don't wait for permission. I scoop her into my arms, pressing her body right against my chest like I can somehow absorb her pain through my skin. She seems so small in my embrace, trembling, her face hidden against my throat as I carry her to the bed and sit with her cradled in my lap.

She doesn't say anything at first. She just lets me hold her. So that's what I do. I hold her tight. I stroke her hair with gentle fingertips. I whisper words of reassurance until the sniffles slow down and then eventually fade.

"I'm sorry," she whispers finally, her voice raw. "I just... I didn't expect to see him. I didn't expect him to say those things. And now he's got the wrong impression. He said that he thinks I'm sleeping with you to be allowed to stay here, and he's probably going to go around and tell everyone, and your whole family is going to think I'm... I'm some kind of..."

"Don't," I growl, my voice rough as gravel. "Don't you fucking finish that sentence, Rose. Nothing could be further from the truth."

Her breath hitches. I pull back just enough to see her face, to tilt her chin up with two fingers so she has no choice but to meet my eyes.

"I don't give a fuck what Chase thinks. Or what anyone else in my family thinks. If any of them think badly of you, it's because they don't know you the way I do. And he's goddamn immature if he thinks I would ask anything of you to stay here. I'd give you the whole fucking world if I could, and I would never ask for a thing in return except your heart. Which I would spend my life protecting."

Her lips part slightly, her eyes wide. I can see the questions swirling in her head. The disbelief, the fear, the hope that maybe I can give her the kind of fierce love she needs that she's too scared to voice.

"You don't have to be afraid of me," I say, softer now. "I know I'm intense, but I've never felt this way before about anybody. I'm not going to hurt you. I'm going to protect you. Worship you."

Her lower lip trembles, and I can't stop myself from reaching up to brush my thumb across it.

"I'm going to give you everything you've ever dreamed of. Not because you ask. Not because I feel like I have to buy your love – something so precious is priceless, anyway. But because the smile on your face will be the only reward I ever want in life."

Rose leans in slightly, just barely. Her breath catches.

And any semblance of control I might have had up until this point snaps.

My lips find hers in a kiss so gentle it feels like a vow. Her hands clutch at my shirt, her fingers twisting the fabric, anchoring herself to me. I feel her exhale into the kiss, feel her soften, melt, open.

Then she kisses me back.

Not tentatively. Not with hesitation.

But like she has been holding back just as much as I have. Like I'm the only thing that makes sense in a world of chaos.

The kiss deepens, growing hotter, hungrier. My control starts to fray at the edges. Her hands tangle in my hair, her body pressing closer to mine, and I groan low in my chest, pulling her tighter. Wanting more. Wanting everything.

Her lips part beneath mine with a soft gasp, and it's all the invitation I need. I devour her.

There's no other word for it.

I kiss her like I've been starving for her – which I have. For months. And now she's finally here in my arms, kissing me back with the same kind of aching desperation I've been living with since the moment I laid eyes on her.

I grip her hips, dragging her even closer, until there isn't a breath of space between us. She moans into my mouth, and my cock twitches in my pants, the hard flesh painfully restrained. Even through our layers of clothing, I can feel the heat of her core against me and it unleashes something feral inside me.

God, the things I want to do to her.

My mind flashes to what I saw on my surveillance camera earlier today. Rose sprawled across my bed, my shirt swallowing her luscious curves, her hand sliding between her thighs, her lips parted with moans of pleasure that I couldn't hear.

The image is burned into my brain.

It's going to ruin me.

I growl against her mouth and kiss her deeper, like I can stake a claim with just my tongue, like I can erase every kiss she's ever experienced and replace it with mine. Only mine.

I need her in ways I can't even name. I need to feel the wet heat of her body as it stretches around me, welcoming me inside, joining us together in a way that goes so much deeper than just the physical.

Her fingers dig into my shoulders, and she whispers my name against my lips – soft and breathless. It rips straight through me, and I tighten my grip on her hips.

But I still make myself stop, just barely.

I tear my lips from hers, panting, my heart slamming against my ribs. I rest my forehead against hers, trying to find something close to control. "Not yet," I whisper, even though every cell in my body is screaming otherwise. "I want you too damn much to mess this up. I need to know you want this too before I go any further."

Her breath catches in her throat, and her eyes grow wide.

But then her gaze drops, and that shimmer of doubt I hate with every part of me creeps into her voice.

"How do I know you won't leave too?" she asks quietly. "What if we... and then you just... go? It hurt enough when Chase made it clear I wasn't enough, but it would hurt even more with you if I... if I actually give myself to you and then you decide you don't want me."

My jaw tightens.

I lift her chin so she has to look at me, and the way her eyes still glisten with tears breaks my heat. "Don't compare me to him, baby. I'm nothing like Chase."

Rose swallows, searching my eyes.

"I'm not going to take what I can and then just disappear, Rose," I tell her, my voice low and firm, showing her how much I mean the words that are coming out of my mouth. "I'm here for every part of you. I want your bad days, your good days, your everything."

I press a kiss to the corner of her mouth, soft but full of promise.

"I've wanted you from the second you walked into my life. I've waited. I've watched. I've burned. And now you're here, and I'm not going to let you go."

Her breath stutters.

"You want to know how serious I am?" I murmur, my lips brushing her cheek. "I want to put a baby in you, Rose. I want to fill you up and watch you swell with my child. I want everyone who looks at you to know exactly who you belong to. And most importantly, I want you to know that we will be bound together for the rest of our years by the tiny little lives I plan to create with you."

Her eyes widen.

"I want forever," I repeat, dead serious. "And I'll spend every damn day proving to you that I mean it."

She stares up at me in shock, lips parted, breathing shallow.

And as I wait for her to respond, everything in me stills, because her next word could be the one that saves me... or ruins me. But either way, I know I'll never stop wanting her.

Chapter Seven

♥

Rose

His words echo in the silence, heavy and earth-shaking.

I stare up at him, my heart pounding so loud it drowns out everything else. My lips part, but no sound comes out. He's watching me like everything hangs on what I'm about to say. Like I could shatter him with whatever comes next.

That kind of pressure should be terrifying, but all I can think about is the way he defended me earlier. The way he held me close and whispered reassuring things to me until I could breathe again.

I've never felt so cherished. So desired.

My heart twists, too full, too raw after everything it's been through the last few days. I've always dreamed of someone looking at me like that. Like I matter. Like I'm not just a passing phase of a placeholder until someone better comes along.

With Chase, I always felt like an option. A backup.

But Damien is different. He's never once looked at me like I was anything less than everything to him.

Even now, he's holding his breath for me.

I want this. I want everything he's promising - the happily ever after with lots of children running around.

My heart knows it. My gut screams it. I've felt the pull toward him since the day we met, and I tried so hard to ignore it. Tried to be loyal to Chase, because he was the one I met first, and I was already his girlfriend by the time I met Damien.

I tried to pretend I didn't notice the way Damien looked at me from across the room, like he already knew I belonged to him, and not his brother.

But I'm done pretending.

My brain, of course, still tries to trip me up.

Is it too soon? What will people say? What will his family think? What if I get hurt again?

I already know what Chase thinks. He made that clear enough today with his cruel words and arrogant smirk.

But when I look up into Damien's eyes - stormy, intense, filled with nothing but devotion - I realize that none of the rest matters. Not the timing. Not the whispers from others. Not even the past.

This man wants to give me everything I've ever dreamed of. And I want him to have all of me.

"You're killing me here, Rose," he says, his voice rough and low, his eyes searching my face. "Say something."

"Make me yours, Damien."

I've barely breathed the words, but I know he hears. He sucks in a sharp breath, his body tensing, his grip on me tightening. His jaw clenches, and for a moment, he looks almost... feral.

Then he moves, flipping us both around, so I'm pinned beneath him on the bed. The movement is so sudden, so unexpected, that I gasp. His weight presses me into the mattress, his gaze burning hotter than a wildfire as he looks down at me, his lips just inches from mine.

"You are mine, Rose," he growls, his voice deep and rasping. "You always have been."

And then his mouth crashes down on mine, hot and hungry. There's no tentative exploration or gentle coaxing.

It's a claiming.

My hands grip his shirt, and his tongue slides along my lips, seeking entrance. The heat of him, the weight of his body, the possessive way he kisses me - it's all almost too much. I feel like my heart might burst. But then he groans, the sound reverberating through his chest, and the only thing in the world that matters is his kiss.

He nips my lower lip, his teeth dragging along the soft flesh before he dives back in, his tongue seeking mine, dancing together in a frenzy. My hands move from his shirt to his neck, to his hair, gripping tightly, as if I can somehow pull him even closer.

We're both breathless and desperate, and it's the hottest moment of my entire life.

I've never felt anything like this. Never experienced such a primal, all-consuming need.

We're both gasping, trying to catch our breath, but the way his hips grind against mine is making it hard to focus on anything but the aching heat pooling between my thighs.

"I'm going to ruin you, Rose," he whispers, his voice harsh, his words a promise. "You'll never want anyone else after this. Only me."

"I've never wanted anyone but you." The words slip out before I can stop them, and the raw truth of them shatters the last bit of restraint we both had.

We move at the same time, my clothes falling away as his fingers tear my shirt over my head. I gasp when his lips find my breasts, licking and sucking and nipping the sensitive skin. He works his way down, peppering kisses along my stomach and down to my hips, pausing only long enough to peel off my panties and toss them aside.

He looks up at me, his eyes wild, his breath coming in harsh pants. "I need to taste you."

I don't have time to respond before he's burying his face between my legs, his tongue darting out to lick my clit.

The shock of pleasure is almost too much. I gasp, arching off the bed, but his hands are on my hips, pinning me in place as he devours me. He groans, the vibration sending another shudder of bliss through my body, and I know that nothing has ever felt this good.

I'm spiraling. Losing control. His tongue circles my clit, and then he plunges a finger deep inside me, making me moan and writhe against his mouth. It feels so good. So perfect.

I'm already close, the pleasure building, when he adds a second finger and curls them, hitting some hidden spot inside me that makes my eyes roll back in my head.

"Please," I gasp, my voice ragged, my body shaking.

He hums against my skin, and the pleasure is so intense I can't hold back. I explode, my orgasm crashing over me like a wave, my entire body spasming with my release.

He doesn't stop, drawing out my pleasure with long, slow licks, his fingers still buried deep inside me.

When he finally pulls away, my whole body feels boneless and sated.

But he's not finished.

He kisses his way back up my body, pausing to suck on my nipples until I'm arching against him, then moves up to my lips, kissing me deeply, letting me taste myself on his tongue.

"I need you, baby," he murmurs, his voice rough with desire. "I need to be inside you. Need to fill you with my seed so you can have a part of me growing inside you for the next nine months."

"Yes," I gasp. "I want that too."

His fingers brush against my bare stomach, almost as if he's already imagining a new life forming inside me. The touch is gentle, so reverent that it almost brings a tear to my eye.

He kisses me again, and I can feel how hard he is.

The heat between us is intense, and when he breaks the kiss, his lips trailing down my neck, his teeth nipping my collarbone, I whimper, desperate for more.

He lifts himself up on one elbow and stares down at me, his gaze fierce and possessive.

"You're mine, Rose," he says, his voice low and deep. "Now and forever."

He kisses me again, his mouth moving over mine, hot and hungry.

"Say it," he commands, his voice rough with desire. "Tell me you're mine."

"I'm yours," I whisper, the words a vow.

His hands roam over my body, exploring every inch of me. He cups my breast, kneading the tender flesh, his thumb teasing my nipple.

I gasp and arch up into him, begging for more.

His touch is driving me wild. Everywhere he touches, my skin burns and aches. I need more. So much more.

"Tell me again," he orders, his lips grazing the shell of my ear.

"I'm yours, Damien," I repeat, my voice breathy.

"Yes you are, baby. And now it's time for me to claim what's mine."

He slides off the bed, leaving me shivering from the sudden lack of contact with him. My body is already begging for more.

But then I realize what he's doing.

He's unbuttoning his shirt.

Oh my god.

Damien is stripping for me.

Every inch of his hard, muscled chest is being revealed to my hungry gaze. His shoulders are broad and strong, his abs rippling with muscle.

And the V that leads down to his pants? Oh, fuck.

He tosses the shirt aside and reaches for his belt, and the anticipation is almost too much. I need him naked, inside me, filling me. Now.

He drops his pants and boxer briefs, and the sight of his cock makes me whimper. It's huge, thick and long and hard, and my body clenches at the thought of him stretching me, filling me.

"I know this is your first time, Rose, and I'll try my best to be gentle. But I can't make any promises. I've been waiting too long for this, and I need you too fucking badly."

His voice is hoarse, his words coming out in a low growl, and the raw honesty and intensity in his eyes is enough to undo me completely.

I no longer have any doubts about us. Not now. I'm meant to be his. I have always been his.

It just took me too damn long to realize it.

Chapter Eight

♥

Damien

As I stand at the edge of the bed, completely naked and with my need completely on display, the way Rose looks at me almost tears me apart. Her gaze roams over every inch of my body, her lips part, her breath catching in her throat. And as much as I need to be inside her right now, I don't want her to stop looking at me like that.

She reaches out tentatively, almost as if she's afraid to touch me. But when her fingertips brush against my abs, I can't stop the growl that emerges from somewhere deep inside me. My dick twitches with a need for her attention, and she gasps softly.

Rose lifts her eyes to mine, and she's got such a pure expression of adoration on her face. Fuck, the way she's looking at me... it makes me want to give her everything. Every piece of myself I've kept locked away. Every breath. Every heartbeat. Every damn drop of me.

"Can I... touch?" she asks, her voice a breathy whisper.

"Fuck, baby. Of course you can touch."

She wraps her hand around my cock, and the moan that comes from me is downright animalistic. She's barely touching me, and I'm already losing it. Her hands are so small, her touch so soft, but I've wanted this for so fucking long.

It's almost too much.

Her hand strokes up and down my length, and I grit my teeth, trying not to lose it right here and now.

She's soft, sweet, careful. She touches me like I'm something holy. Like she's worshipping me with her touch. I've had women chase my money, my power, my name - but no one's ever touched me like this. Like I'm the prize. And all it does is make me need to claim her even more. All I want to do is mark. Brand. Bury myself so deep inside her that she forgets there was ever a time she didn't belong to me.

As her gentle hand moves over my flesh, coaxing drops of arousal from the tip, all I can think about is how she'll look with my ring on her finger. My baby growing in her belly. My seed dripping from between her thighs.

I want to feel her tremble when I slide into her. I want to hear her whimpering my name like a prayer - like I'm the only god she's ever worshipped. Because I am. I will be. From this moment on.

Slowly, she leans forward, bringing her mouth so close to the head of my dick that I can feel her breath skimming over the sensitive flesh. But she pauses, looking up at me, seeking permission to continue.

"Baby, if you put that beautiful mouth anywhere near me, I won't be able to stop myself."

She blinks at me, those big, innocent eyes wide and curious.

"You won't have to stop yourself, Damien," she whispers. "I don't want you to."

Then, without breaking eye contact, she flicks her tongue across the swollen head, and it's like a fuse has been lit.

With a snarl, I grab her and toss her onto her back on the bed. She lets out a startled squeak, but there's no time to worry if I scared her.

Because my hands are on her thighs, pushing them open, spreading her wide. Her pussy is pink and glistening with need, and the scent of her desire is almost enough to push me over the edge.

My fingers dig into her flesh as I stare down at her. "I can't be gentle right now, Rose. You're driving me crazy."

She reaches out and pulls me toward her, her legs wrapping around my waist, her heels digging into my ass.

"Don't be," she breathes. "I want you, Damien. I want all of you. Don't hold back."

She doesn't know she's feeding the beast inside me. The part of me that needs to possess her. This isn't about sex. This is about putting my scent on her skin, my taste on her tongue, and my baby in her womb. So no one ever fucking doubts who she belongs to again.

I reach down, sliding a hand between our bodies, pressing a finger deep inside her slick little hole. She's so tight that she feels snug even around that single digit, and I already know it's going to feel like heaven when I slide inside her.

She gasps, writhing beneath me as I add a second finger to the mix, stretching her, preparing her body to take mine.

"Who does this pretty little pussy belong to, Rose?" I ask, my voice hoarse with an overwhelming need for her.

"It's yours, Damien," she moans, her eyes fluttering shut as she surrenders to my touch.

I push a third finger into her welcoming heat, and she lets out a gasp. Her tight inner walls flutter around the digits, and I grit my teeth, imagining how it's going to feel when she's stretched around me.

"You were made to be mine, Rose," I tell her. "Every inch of your soft, sweet body. Every heartbeat. Every breath. I'll carve my fucking name into your soul if I have to. But you will never, ever doubt my love for you."

"Yes," she breathes. "Damien…"

I withdraw my fingers and wrap a hand around my cock, stroking it through her wetness. She whimpers, her hips arching up, seeking more.

"Tell me you want this," I growl, nudging her entrance.

"Please, Damien." Her voice is a needy whine, her eyes dark with desire. "Make me yours."

With a groan, I thrust inside her, burying myself to the hilt in one powerful stroke. She cries out, her nails digging into my back, her legs locking around me.

It's all too much. The feel of her heat wrapped around me. The taste of her skin. The scent of her desire. The way she's clinging to me, begging me to make her mine.

I can't hold back anymore.

With a growl, I pull out and slam back in, over and over, claiming her with every thrust.

"Damien," she moans, her hips rocking, matching the pace I set. "It's so good. Oh my god, please, don't stop."

I'm lost in the feel of her. The pleasure is like nothing I've ever experienced before.

My fingers grip her hips, lifting them off the bed slightly as I pound into her, driving myself deeper, harder, faster.

The world around us fades away until all that's left is the sound of her soft cries and the feel of her body trembling beneath me.

It's too much. Too intense.

My body tightens, and I know I'm close.

"Come for me, Rose," I rasp, my voice raw with need. "I want to feel you come on my cock. I need to know you're mine."

I reach between our bodies, my fingers seeking her clit. Her eyes flutter closed, and her head falls back, exposing the delicate column of her throat.

I lower my mouth, biting down on the soft skin, marking her.

Her body clenches around me, her inner walls squeezing me tightly as she tumbles over the edge.

"Yes," I groan, my hips jerking. "Fuck, baby. I'm going to breed you, Rose. Going to turn you into the fertile little goddess you were always meant to be for me."

The words spill out of me, and they feel right. Fated.

She was born to be mine, and I was born to be hers.

As the orgasm slams through me, I bury myself inside her, holding her body tightly to mine as my release floods her. I fill her with every last drop, and it's a primal, possessive satisfaction, knowing that it might be the start of a new life. A future together.

She's breathing hard, her body trembling, her heart racing. Her skin is flushed, and her hair is a tangled mess. She looks thoroughly wrecked.

And so fucking gorgeous.

I've never seen anything so beautiful.

"I love you," she murmurs, her voice filled with awe.

"I love you, too, baby."

I press a gentle kiss to her lips, and it feels like a promise. A vow.

This woman is my forever.

My everything.

And I'm never letting her go.

Chapter Nine

Damien

She's still asleep. Sprawled across my sheets like a dream that's come true, her dark hair wild around her face, her cheeks still flushed from everything we did last night.

After everything I did to her.

Rose has got that soft, wrecked look - like her body is still trying to process all the ways I claimed it. And her lips... fuck. Swollen from my kisses, parted just enough for those quiet little breaths that make me want to wake her and make her scream all over again.

I could watch her like this forever, though.

This right here? It's everything I ever wanted. Everything I never knew I needed until she walked into my life six months ago with that shy little smile and those eyes that always held me captivated. And now that I've got her, I'm never letting her go.

I'll build her a life so solid, so safe, so full of love that she'll never question her worth again. And if anyone tries to hurt her... hell, I'll burn the entire fucking world down and salt the ashes. That's not an exaggeration.

It's a goddamn promise.

I'm already picturing it - the house, the baby in her arms, my ring on her finger. I want all of it. Her belly round with my child, her smile brighter than the sun because she knows she's mine and she's loved unconditionally.

Rose stirs slightly, her lashes fluttering, but she doesn't wake. I pull the blanket higher over her shoulder, hating the thought of her getting cold, and brush my lips tenderly against her temple.

But then the quiet morning is shattered by a loud banging on the front door. The noise rips through the house like a threat. Rose blinks awake, groggy and confused, and starts to sit up.

"No, baby," I murmur, smoothing my hand over her back. "Stay in bed. I've got it."

She nods, trusting me completely, and curls back up beneath the blanket. I pull on a pair of sweats and I'm already halfway down the stairs by the time the next round of pounding hits.

Who the fuck is banging on my door at ten a.m. on a Saturday?

I wrench the door open, and there they are.

Chase. And our mother.

Of course.

I don't even bother with a greeting. "What do you want?" I demand, directing my words towards my youngest brother.

But Mom's mouth is already opening, her face a mixture of disappointment and annoyance. "Damien, how dare you? How could you betray your brother like this?"

Chase stands beside her, arms crossed, with a smug look on the face like he's the cat who got the fucking cream.

"Betray him?" I scoff, not even bothering to open the front door enough to let them in. If this is how they are going to treat me, I'm not sure I want either of them in my house right now. "You want to talk about betrayal, maybe ask your golden boy what really happened."

Chase glares at me. "You stole my girl."

"No," I growl. "I didn't steal anything. You lost her all on your own, Chase. You treated her like a goddamn object. Like she should just spread her legs and be grateful you gave her the time of day. You pressured her. Tried to push her into something she wasn't ready for. And when your manipulation didn't work, you got rid of her like a piece of trash. And now you have the fucking nerve to turn up on my doorstep and accuse me of taking her from you?"

The rage boils in my veins, hot and relentless, like a fuse burning down fast. My fists clench at my sides, my jaw tight enough to crack. I've spent months watching Rose shrink beneath the weight of Chase's selfishness, biting her tongue, pretending she was fine. And now he stands here, smug and self-righteous, rewriting history to paint himself at the victim? I want to put my fist through a wall - or better yet, through his face. Because no one gets to hurt her and walk away clean. Not anymore.

Mom gasps. "Chase? Is that true?"

He shifts uncomfortably but doesn't answer.

I look directly at her. "Nothing happened between me and Rose until after Chase had ended things with her. There was a flood at her apartment, and she needed somewhere to stay for a while until it's fixed. But I've always loved her, Mom. Ever since I first met her. I held back because I didn't want to hurt my brother, but now she's single, I refuse to hold back any longer."

"Love her?" Mom repeats, like she's struggling to understand the meaning of my words.

"Yes, I love Rose," I say, my voice rough with emotion. "I've always wanted her. And now that I have her, I've got an entire damn future planned out for us. A home. A family. This isn't just a fling. I want forever with Rose."

There's a beat of stunned silence.

Chase is scowling, arms still crossed. I've got no idea if he's mad at me for calling him out, or because he genuinely believes that I stole Rose from him. But I can't bring myself to care.

Mom turns to him slowly. "You told me he stole her from you. That she cheated on you with your own brother?"

Chase remains silent and looks away.

"Oh my god," she says, her voice rising in pitch. "I raised you better than this, Chase."

Chase mutters something under his breath, but she doesn't even look at him anymore. She just shakes her head like she's seeing him clearly for the first time.

And maybe she is.

I take a step towards them, letting all the fury and protective energy I'm holding coil just beneath the surface.

"I won't let either of you come here and make Rose feel like she's done something wrong. She's been through enough. And if you can't treat her with the respect she deserves, you're not welcome near either of us."

"Damien..." Mom tries again, her voice quieter this time. Softer.

I lift a hand, not to cut her off, but to slow things down. "I'm not trying to shut you out, Mom. But you have to understand... Rose means everything to me. And I won't let anyone hurt her again. Not even family."

Her expression shifts - just slightly - but I see it. Maybe she hears the conviction in my voice, or maybe it's the rawness I can't hide when I talk about Rose. Either way, I believe she understands how serious I am.

"I didn't know," she says after a moment, glancing sideways at Chase. "I only heard his side of things. But if what you are saying is true..." She turns to chase fully now, eyes narrowing. "We're going to go home and have a conversation, young man. And you're going to stay away from Rose and Damien unless you've got something respectful and mature to say."

Chase's mouth opens, but Mom cuts him off this time. "Enough. I don't want to hear any more lies."

Then she looks back at me - tired, but sincere. "You take care of that girl, Damien. She clearly means a lot to you."

"She's everything to me," I say simply.

Mom nods once, then turns and heads down the steps. Chase follows in sullen silence.

I wait until Mom's car disappears down the road before I close the door behind them, exhaling a slow breath.

When I turn around, my breath catches.

Rose is sitting at the top of the stairs, wrapped in my blanket, and if I'm not mistaken, beneath it, I see the collar of one of my shirts peeking out. Her eyes are wide and glassy, full of so many emotions I can't even name them all.

"You heard all of that," I say, my throat tight.

She nods slowly, then rises and makes her way down the stairs towards me.

Chapter Ten

Rose

My bare feet are silent against the steps as I move towards him, the blanket trailing behind me. Damien doesn't move, doesn't even breathe. His eyes stay locked on mine, like he's afraid one wrong move will make me run just like I tried to do after the last confrontation with Chase.

But I'm not afraid.

Not anymore.

Not after what I just witnessed.

The way he stood there - shoulders squared, jaw tight, voice low and deadly - defending me like I'm something precious. The way he told them the truth, without hesitation. The way he didn't flinch, didn't falter, even when his mother - his own damn mother - looked at him with disappointment.

He chose me.

Without question, without shame.

He stood between me and the world and made it very clear that I'm his.

And while I'm so happy that his mother believed him, and it doesn't seem like my relationship with Damien is going to ruin his relationship with the other people in his life who love him most, the way he was willing to cut ties if he had to, for me...

It's everything.

"Rose..." His voice is a low rasp when I reach the bottom step. "Say something. Please."

Instead of answering, I step right into his space and wrap my arms around his waist. He exhales a shuddering breath and folds his arms around me like he's afraid I might vanish if he doesn't hold me tight enough.

"I'm sorry that you had to find out he was telling lies about you, Rose. But I promise I will do whatever it takes to make sure nobody believes a damn word out of his mouth."

A soft smile tugs at my lips. "I know," I whisper against his chest. "I love you."

His arms squeeze tighter. "I love you too, baby. So damn much."

"I don't care what anyone else thinks," I go on, my voice trembling with all the emotions bubbling to the surface. "You didn't steal me. You just showed me what love was really supposed to feel like."

He tilts my chin up, eyes burning into mine. "And I plan to spend the rest of my life showing you."

"I know," I whisper.

His jaw tics. "I didn't want you to hear all of that. About the trouble my brother was trying to cause."

"But I'm glad I did," I say softly. "Because now I know. I know how much I matter to you. I know I'm not just some fling or some stolen prize. I'm yours. And you're mine."

His eyes darken, something primal flickering there. "Say that again."

"You're mine too, Damien."

He groans like the words physically affect him. Then he cups my face with both hands, eyes full of reverence and heat all at once.

"I've been yours since the very first moment I saw you. I've just been waiting for you to realize it." His lips quirk up into a sexy grin, and my heart flutters wildly in my chest.

I lean into his touch. "I'm sorry. Let me make it up to you." I place my hand on his bare abs, savoring the feel of his hard muscle and soft skin beneath my fingertips. Then my hand trails lower, to the waistband of his sweatpants.

The air between us shifts. Thickens. Sparks.

He lowers his mouth to mine and kisses me like a man unraveling before I even get a chance to pull down his pants and free the hard length that's creating a tent in the fabric. Instead, my arms go around his neck, and I melt into him, letting him take control for now.

His hands are already under the blanket, pushing it from my shoulders, his growl low and full of heat when he sees I'm wearing nothing but his shirt. "Jesus, baby. Are you trying to kill me?"

I grin, breathless. "Only a little."

He leans in, his lips brushing my ear. "It's almost as sexy as the first time I saw you wearing one of my shirts."

I blink, confused. "What do you mean? You've never seen me wearing..."

He cuts me off with a wicked grin. "I have, baby. I'm guessing you didn't realize I've got a security camera set up in my bedroom. I put it there because of the safe I've got hidden in that room, but yesterday, I caught sight of something delicious on the feed while I was stuck in a very boring meeting."

My stomach drops, and a burning sensation rushes up my neck to flood my cheeks. "You... saw me?" I ask, my heart hammering in my chest.

I try to squirm out of his embrace, but he catches me gently, firmly.

"No, no, baby. Don't run. Don't ever be embarrassed about that. It was the single hottest thing I've ever seen in my life. You, needing me like that, without even realizing I was watching, it wrecked me, Rose."

I swallow hard. "And... did you like what you saw?"

"So fucking much. I was so damn hard the whole time. And the moment the meeting was over, I was coming straight back home, ready to fuck you into the mattress. But Chase was here, so I had to wait a little longer before I could claim what's mine."

The flush burns even hotter, but it's not embarrassment. It's the memory of what happened last night. What I'm hoping is about to happen again right now.

He sees it, reads the desire in my expression, and he sweeps me up into his arms and carries me to the couch like I weigh nothing.

"The bed is too far away," he rasps. "I need you now."

And when he lays me out and strips that shirt away from my body, the look in his eyes is enough to make my heart stutter.

Like I'm his whole world.

Like I'm his everything.

But I want to make him feel the same too. So I move up into a sitting position, running my hands over his chest while I lean in and press gentle kisses against his neck.

"When you said that you're mine too, does that mean I can do whatever I want to you, Damien?"

He tilts his head to the side, exposing his throat to my kisses, and a low growl rumbles through him. "So long as it ends up with me filling your fertile little body with a load of my cum, you can do anything, baby."

My body shivers with delight.

"Good. Because there's something I've been wanting to do to you ever since I first saw you naked yesterday. But don't worry. I'll make sure it ends the way you want it to."

I slide down from the couch and settle on my knees between his thighs, licking my lips as I see the outline of his cock straining against his pants. He reaches down and frees himself, and the thick length bounces against his belly.

His gaze burns into me as I lower my mouth and wrap my lips around the spongy head, tasting his salty pre-cum. His eyes are glued to me, and he looks like a man on fire. Like he's already about to lose his mind.

I lick up the underside of his cock and swirl my tongue around the head, then sink back down, taking as much of him into my mouth as I can. It's not even half, so I wrap my hand around the base and start pumping in rhythm with my mouth.

"Fuck, Rose. Your mouth feels so good, baby."

I moan, sucking him harder, deeper, loving the feel of his shaft thickening in my mouth. Loving the way his hands thread through my hair, tugging just hard enough to send a rush of wetness between my thighs.

He's panting, and it sounds so sexy, knowing I'm the one doing that to him. The powerful Damien Knight, losing his damn mind because of what I'm doing with my mouth.

"You keep sucking me like that, and I'm going to blow," he growls, and the warning in his voice has another rush of arousal flooding me.

I'm about to tell him it's okay, but his hands tighten in my hair, and he pulls me off his cock.

"No," he grunts. "As much as I'd love to finish in your mouth, I'm not going to waste a drop of my cum. Not today."

He pulls me up off the floor and into his lap, then he's kissing me like a starving man. My thighs clench, and my whole body feels tight and aching and so, so desperate.

"Slide down on my cock, baby," he demands, his voice rough. "I need to be inside you already."

"Yes," I breathe.

Then I'm shifting into position and sinking down onto him. He grabs my hips and pulls me down faster, harder, until his entire thick length is buried inside me.

We both cry out, and his lips crash into mine again, swallowing our moans.

I start riding him, and his hands stay on my hips, helping me set the pace. But the longer I go, the less I need his help. He leans back, watching me take him, and the intensity in his eyes sends another pulse of desire through me.

"Ride that cock, baby. Show me how much you love having my dick buried inside you."

I gasp, moving faster. My fingers curl against his chest, leaving faint red lines in his skin, and he growls, lifting his hips off the couch, driving his cock into me even deeper.

"Damien, yes!"

His name turns into a strangled cry as he thrusts up into me, hard and fast, and I can already feel my climax rushing up to meet me.

"Oh god, I'm close."

"Me too, baby."

"Don't stop."

"Never."

I'm bouncing in his lap now, chasing my release. It's right there, coiled inside me, waiting.

"Touch yourself, Rose," he growls. "Rub your clit and come on my cock. I want to watch you come undone for me."

I reach down and rub frantic circles over my clit, and it's all it takes to send me over the edge. I cry out, clenching tight around him as my orgasm rushes through me, wave after wave of pleasure.

"Fuck yes, that's it, baby," Damien snarls, still thrusting up into me. He's so big and deep, and his movements are only drawing out my orgasm.

"I'm going to fill your little pussy with cum, Rose. Do you want that, baby? Do you want me to breed you?"

"Yes," I gasp, the pleasure making me dizzy. "Yes, please. Give me your cum."

His eyes are wild, and his grip on my hips is punishing. His next thrust is so hard, I can't hold back the scream.

He does it again, and this time, the scream is his name.

"Damien! Fuck!"

He slams up into me a final time, his whole body tensing, and his cock jerks hard as his release floods me. I can feel him painting my insides, feel his seed seeping into me, and the thought makes me shiver and tremble.

He holds me there, his cock buried deep inside me, his hands on my hips and his forehead pressed to mine.

"Rose, baby. Jesus Christ."

"Yeah," I agree, breathless.

His chest rises and falls, and he's looking at me with so much reverence, I can hardly stand it.

"You are so damn perfect. Every single thing about you."

He wraps his arms around me, holding me close, and we sit there for a long moment, catching our breath.

"I'm going to miss this when it's time for me to go back to my apartment," I say, once I've recovered.

"Fuck that," he growls. "This is your home now, baby. You're not going anywhere. You belong here. With me."

I smile, warmth blooming in my chest. "You mean that?"

"Of course I mean it, Rose. You're everything I've always wanted. And I'm not giving that up now."

He leans in and brushes his lips over mine. "This is only the beginning for us, baby. There's a whole life ahead of us, and I want you by my side through all of it."

I lean in and kiss him, feeling giddy and light and happier than I've ever been. "I'm not going anywhere, Damien. Ever. I'm yours. Forever."

"Damn right you are," he growls. Then his lips are on mine, and I'm being lifted and carried to the bed, and my heart is full to bursting, because no matter what life throws our way, we'll face it together.

Epilogue

Rose

Seven months later:

Seven months pregnant.

That's what the calendar says, and my aching back agrees. My ankles are swollen, my boobs feel like they've doubled in size, and if one more person tells me I'm glowing, I might actually cry. Or scream.

But let's be honest. I'll probably do both.

The only thing getting me through today is the promise of Damien walking through that door. He's been in meetings all day, so I've barely even been able to speak to him on the phone, and my heart misses him.

I shift on the couch, trying to find a position that doesn't feel like I'm being crushed from the inside out. My belly is round and heavy, jutting out in front of me like a monument to exactly how effective Damien's possessive, primal devotion turned out to be.

The man said he was going to put a baby in me, and wow. Mission definitely accomplished. He was so successful that there are two little ones fighting for space in my belly.

Still, as much as I wanted this, today I just feel... blah. Puffy. Tired. Huge. I glance down at the oversized hoodie stretched over my bump and let out a soft sigh. It's Damien's, of course. Somehow that makes me feel a little better. A little closer to him.

I miss him.

The front door clicks open.

I sit up a little straighter - or try to, anyway - as heavy footsteps sound across the floor. And then I see him.

Damien.

My heart does that ridiculous flutter it's never once skipped whenever I see him, even now, even after all this time. His short hair is as immaculate as ever, but his jaw is dusted with stubble. He's still wearing his suit, although his tie has been loosened and the top couple of buttons have been popped open. His eyes lock on me the moment he steps into the room.

And then he stops dead in his tracks.

"Fuck me," he breathes. "Look at you."

I blink. "What?"

He strides forward like a man possessed, dropping his keys on the coffee table and shrugging out of his suit jacket without even taking his eyes off me. His gaze is dark and hungry, raking over every inch of me like I'm the most beautiful thing he's ever seen.

I try to smile, but it's sheepish at best. "I feel like a beached whale."

"You look like a fucking goddess." He's already kneeling in front of the couch before I can respond, one big palm sliding over the crest of my belly like it's sacred. "My fertile goddess."

His voice drops to a growl, and I swear I can feel it between my legs.

"Damien..." I whisper, but it comes out more like a whimper.

He lifts the hem of the hoodie just enough to press a kiss to the bare curve of my stomach. Then another. Then one just a little lower.

"Do you even know what you do to me?" he murmurs, his lips brushing my skin. "Every time I come home and see you like this...

round with my twin babies, glowing with my love, wrapped in my clothes... fuck, Rose. It makes me want to worship you."

I run my fingers through his hair, trembling a little beneath the reverent way he touches me.

He lifts his eyes to mine, dark and burning with need.

"Let me worship you, baby. Every inch. Let me remind you exactly who you are to me."

And as he presses another kiss to my belly and starts trailing lower, I nod, breath caught in my throat, already aching for what I know is coming next.

With his eyes on mine, he loops a strong arm beneath me and lifts my ass off the couch just enough that he can pull my yoga pants and panties down with his free hand. Then he tosses them aside and slides his hands over my stomach, caressing it gently, and lowers his mouth to the heat between my thighs. My swollen stomach makes it impossible to see his head there, but god, I can sure feel him. His tongue traces the seam of my lips, then slips between them, circling my clit.

"Oh, Damien."

"You taste so fucking sweet, baby."

He groans against me, and the vibration sends a pulse of pleasure through me. His mouth closes over my clit and he sucks, swirling his tongue over it, and I can't hold back the moan. I instinctively reach towards him, wanting to grip his hair and pull him closer, but I can't reach him around my huge baby bump. So instead, I place my hands over his, where they rest on my stomach, both of us feeling every little movement coming from within.

He eats me with single-minded focus, licking and sucking and devouring every inch of me like a starving man.

It's not long before I'm shaking, the pleasure building deep inside me, threatening to snap.

"I'm close," I gasp, my toes curling.

His mouth doesn't let up, his tongue working furiously, sending me spiraling. My back arches, and I cry out as the first wave hits me.

"Damien!"

It's almost painful, the intensity, and I grip his hands hard enough to leave little crescent-shaped marks on his skin. He's moaning, still licking and sucking at my pussy, dragging the orgasm out as long as he can, until my legs are trembling and the room is spinning and I don't know if I can handle any more.

He gives me one final, slow lick, and then he's pulling himself up onto the couch and wrapping one arm around me, pulling me close against his side. His other hand is back on my stomach, as if he can't stop touching the evidence of his claim on me... and I love it.

He kisses my hair and I rest my cheek on his shoulder, and for a while, we just sit there in silence, breathing each other in, hearts beating in sync.

Then I smile and glance up at him. "Thank you. That was exactly what I needed."

"Anything for my fertile little goddess," he says, one corner of his lip curling up into a playful grin. "I need to keep you sweet so you'll let me knock you up again as soon as possible once these little ones are born. I hope you didn't think the need to claim your womb was just a onetime deal?"

My heart skips, and I grin, pressing my face against his chest. "No," I say softly. "I had a feeling it wasn't."

"Good." He kisses the top of my head, and I can feel the smile on his lips.

"I love you," I whisper.

"Love you too, baby. So much."

And when he pulls back and claims my lips in a long, lingering kiss, I believe it. I feel it.

And I'm ready to spend the rest of my life making him feel the same.

About the Author

♥

Welcome to my wild, wicked world of *over-the-top, heart-pounding instalove*. I write fast-paced, **spicy age gap novellas** that don't waste time. They are just pure heat, obsession, and unapologetic desire from page one. If you're into dominant older heroes, eager younger heroines, and deliciously deviant themes like **breeding** and **lactation**, you're in the right place.

These days, all my stories revolve around one irresistible idea: **men who fall fast, fall hard, and never let go**. Think possessive, primal, borderline unhinged alphas who'd burn the world down for their girl. They're obsessed, they're intense, and yes, more than one has been lovingly described as a full-blown *caveman* by reviewers.

So whether you're here for the age gaps, the obsession, or the kind of heat that leaves scorch marks, you're in the right place. Get comfortable. It's about to get *feral*.

Find Willow online at https://allmylinks.com/willow-watkins